MW01520458

A Pride Anthem

Rob Browatzke

COVER PHOTOGRAPHY
ALEX BISCHOFF

Jake was dead. There was no denying it. His funeral, five years earlier, had been standing-room only, and his ashes were in a black urn on the shelf. That was the only sign of Jake in the office though. No pictures of Jake could be found on the walls, either here or at home. His name wouldn't be found on any of the papers that piled up on Ben's desk, or on any of the awards and commendations framed on the walls. He was dead, and best forgotten. For the most part, Ben did remember to forget him, and so it came as a complete surprise when Ben woke up to find Jake standing over him.

Jake had died the way many gay men die. No, not AIDS. Many stories exist where gay men die from AIDS, but this is not one of them. No, what Jake had died from had been loneliness. Loneliness, you say? Yes. It is indeed deadly, and many gay men die from it. Sometimes, that manifests as overdose; sometimes, as suicide. In Jake's case, it had been getting behind the wheel while stinking drunk and wrapping the car around a lamp post. Ben had identified the body, because even though they'd been broken up for two years, their lives were permanently intertwined in the club they owned together. Yes, Ben had gone down to the morgue, identified the body, and certainly never expected to wake up at five in the morning, years later, and see Jake standing at the foot of the bed.

Except, wait! Ben wasn't in bed. He had fallen asleep on the couch in his office again, something that happened more and more often. Still, home or office, the long-deceased didn't suddenly appear. Was he dreaming? Blinking and pinching himself didn't change anything. Jake was standing there looking just like he had in life. Although much more translucent, and had he always had a blue glow? Probably not.

So, he was a ghost. That was clear. Ben didn't believe in ghosts, or God, or much of anything anymore really. Still, he did believe in what he saw, and he was seeing Jake's ghost.

Had he been thinking of Jake when he fell asleep? No. He never thought about Jake. Jake was long dead, and by the end of a Friday night on Pride weekend, Ben felt pretty dead himself. When the DJ cut the music at three, Ben had emerged from his office long enough to flood the space with light, sending all the gays scurrying for the exits. Just like happened every weekend. And just like every weekend for the past five years, Ben hadn't been thinking about Jake when he did it.

He hadn't been thinking about Jake's chin dimple. He hadn't been thinking about Jake's sculpted torso. He hadn't been thinking about the way Jake's pale green eyes stared out from behind his black-rimmed glasses. No, when Ben fell asleep, after the last customer and staff went out into the night before Pride, Ben hadn't been thinking about Jake at all.

“Hello Benjamin,” the ghost said.

Yes. It was Jake for sure. No one else called him Benjamin. Not even his parents called him Benjamin, even when he was a kid and in trouble. Benjamin was the name on his birth certificate, but it had always been Ben. Except to Jake. God forbid Ben ever call him Jacob though!

"You're a ghost."

"You're observant."

"Why are you here?"

"I'm here to warn you, Benjamin. I'm not the last ghost you're going to see tonight. You'll be visited by three more."

"That sounds very familiar," Ben said. "Why?"

"I'm dead," Jake said. "You're not. Tomorrow, it's Pride."

"Meh," Ben said. He hated Pride. He was gay and sure, he was proud, but he hated Pride. He ran a gay club, and sure, it was what it was, especially on Pride weekend, but he hated Pride. Even counting the money didn't bring him joy. It was just money. Tomorrow, there would be another party; next year, there'd be another Pride. It was just another day.

"Not meh. It's important, Benjamin, and it's important you remember why."

"Just tell me then and let me get back to sleep. Why should I care?"

"There's rules. I can't tell you. I can only warn you to pay attention. It's important for you though, Benjamin, that you learn."

"Lessons from the ghost of a man who drank himself to death."

"That wasn't about you, you know, or the club, or the break-up, or anything. I was just... lonely."

Bingo, Ben thought. "Still, my life doesn't need lessons from the dead."

"You're sleeping alone on the couch in our office on what should be the biggest celebration in your year."

There wasn't much to say to that, Ben thought. It was very true. Even dead, Jake scored points.

"Three more ghosts will come tonight, Benjamin. Please, be open to what they show you. I would rest easier knowing you were happier."

"My happiness wasn't much of a concern when you left me," Ben said, "or when you got behind that wheel."

Jake flinched. "I can't argue with that," he said. "I carry those chains all the time." And suddenly, Ben could see the chains, glowing and thick. They hung around Jake's shoulders, like Ben's arms once had. They wrapped around Jake's body, like Ben once had. There were so many of them. How was Jake even standing? The chains hung on his forearms as if he was trying to bring in all the groceries in one trip, and there was nothing Ben could do to help. "My time here is nearly done, Benjamin. I do not think I'll be able to see you again."

The weight of that suddenly hit Ben like one of those ghost chains. He was seeing Jake again. Jake, who was dead, yes, but Jake, who he had loved.

Ben jumped to his feet. "Can't you stay though? I miss you," he called out, stepping forward to hug the ghost, but only grasping air.

Jake was gone. Again.

"Three more," Jake's voice said, fainter. "Listen, Benjamin. And Benjamin, I love you."

"Jake!"

No answer came. Ben sat down on the couch and started to cry.

It had been a normal Friday, up until Ben woke up to his dead partner's spectral apparition staring down at him. As normal as any Friday can be. As normal as any Friday the night before the year's annual Pride festivities can be. Which is to say, not particularly normal at all. But while the Gs and the Ls and the Bs and the Ts and the every other letters danced and pranced and drank and sank into sweet oblivion, it had been a normal Friday for Ben.

That normal Friday consisted of hiding in the safe space of his office as long as possible. His office, with its double desks piled high in papers, walls plastered in old posters and pictures, shelving filled with the flotsam and jetsam accumulated from years in a gay bar – everything from microphones to feather boas to bottles of booze randomly placed – his office was an island of calm. Calm, you say? Yes, we know. It looked chaotic, to an outside eye anyway. We see why you're confused, but compare it to what happened beyond the double-locked door: a sea of writhing bodies and thriving drama, where break-ups and make-ups and make-outs and dancing and drinking and drugging happened in every corner, where bathroom stalls were for bumps and bjs and only rarely for actual bathrooming, where drag queens wove among the crowd, freed from the arbitrarily assigned roles of either gender (and exercising that freedom by grabbing crotches at will before helping themselves to the drinks of the stunned stranger), where everywhere you looked, someone was taking a selfie, or taking a shot, or taking a chance, where everywhere you looked, someone was laughing or smiling or crying, but living. Yes, the chaos of the office was indeed an oasis compared to the tumult outside. Here, Ben worked up the strength to slap on the smile and do another round with the crowd, shaking hands and hugging and making small talk with the twinks and the bears and the dykes and the queens before running back into his shelter.

It hadn't always been like that, but it had been, for a while now. Since Jake died. Maybe before even. The staff knew when to bother him, and when to leave him be; the customers did too. He was trying, truly trying, but he was tired, truly tired. At least he had Bobby as an assistant manager, reliable, dedicated.

When the lights came on and the music faded into blessed silence, it was Bobby who herded the customers out the door, sending them out into the warm June night to frolic in the streets. It was Bobby who made sure the staff restored the club to some semblance of cleanliness. It was Bobby who brought in the cash drawers for Ben to count.

It was Bobby who went to Ben, just before he left and said, “are you sure you won't join us tomorrow?”

He knew Ben wouldn't but every year he asked.

“Meh,” was Ben's only reply.

“It's Pride though. The staff would love to have you come join us at the parade.”

“The parade! Don't get me started on the parade! It's too commercial, too corporate! Where's the heart that used to be there? It's not the Pride it once was, let me tell you!”

Picture Ben, if you will, saying this, like a cartoon old man waving his fist at a cloud. That’s how we see it too, and we know, like you know, that the cloud doesn’t care. Ben too knew the cloud didn’t care, and Ben also knew that the cloud would be replaced by another and then another and then another.

“A drink in the beer gardens after then? Just an appearance?”

“Someone has to take care of things here, Bobby, while you're all off enjoying yourselves. These nights don't just happen.”

“You know I know that, boss. You know I care about this place almost as much as you do.”

This place.

Good Judy's had been their dream, you see. His and Jake's. Seventeen years ago, they'd bought it from its old owner. Seventeen years? Really? Could it really be that long? Where had the intervening years gone? How did time move so fast? Ben had been younger, so much younger, and probably far less wise, and probably far happier because of it. But yes, this Pride night, when Ben awoke to Jake’s ghost, was seventeen years after they bought Good Judy’s from Old Lady Paull, for whom they had both worked for years. They had bought it, drunk on love and excitement and gin, to make it their own. Jake had been working there for three years, Ben longer. They had met while working there, had started dating while working there. And when the big boss decided to retire, they pooled their savings, and took a chance.

And for twelve years, they ran it together, and every night was something new and wonderful, and it soon became the #1 drinking spot for the whole city, gay, straight, and everyone in between. And Pride was always a part of that. A big part. A fun part. Even when Jake decided that the romantic relationship between them had run its course, Pride was still something to look forward to.

But now, Jake was dead, and Good Judy's was doing fine on its own, and it didn't really need Ben, and Ben didn't really need it, and he certainly didn't need some parade of corporate logos. The council that put it all together was a bunch of kids! Where were they when Ben and Jake were building up the bar? Or all the years before? What did they know about hardship or struggle or anything? All they knew was businesses falling over each other to show their support to the almighty rainbow flag. Back then, they were a true community, allied together in the fight against AIDS or the fight for political change; now, identity politics had shattered the unity of that community, and everyone was wrong, and everyone was in it for themselves, and what even was a gender-fluid pansexual anyway?

Meh, Pride indeed!

“It's just a place,” he told Bobby, “and tomorrow's just another day. You and the staff do your thing, but be on time, and ready to work. Bills pile up, and tomorrow's a good time to pay some off!"

With that, Ben rounded the corner, and BAM. "What -?" he said, stepping back from the person he had just run into.

"Oh," Bobby said, grinning, "by the way, Kevin stuck around to say goodnight." Bobby took off in a jog, leaving Ben face to face with Kevin.

Kevin was a regular customer, and too damn handsome for his own good. Ben glanced down. He didn't like making eye contact with Kevin, too young, too handsome, too perfect a smile. It was the curls, Ben decided, that really made him handsome – dark brown and kind of floppy, or was it the eyes – pale blue and yet still warm? Or maybe the skin that looked like it had never seen a blemish? Or the way his jeans clung to his incredible thighs? Or…

"I just wanted to say thanks for another good night," Kevin said. Even his voice was flawless.

"Glad you enjoyed yourself," Ben said, trying to shift into people-mode. Everyone *should* have been gone though. People-mode *should* have ended at three. Damn interfering Bobby.

"You always throw a good party. Are you going to watch the parade tomorrow?"

"Meh."

"I've never seen you out at Pride festivities, come to think of it. Not your thing?"

"Too corporate, too chaotic, too much of everything."

"Too bad. I thought we could maybe watch it together."

Warnings screamed in Ben's mind. Too young! Too hot! Too soon! Too drunk! "I won't be there," he said, harder and stronger than he'd meant. Shifting back into work-mode, he slapped on a smile and continued, "I'll be here though later. Party of the year, of course. Make sure you say hi. I'll get you a drink." He could feel how fake the smile was, a grin plastered so broadly across his face that he was surprised the top of his head didn't simply fall off; surely Kevin must have noticed how fake it was too, everyone must have noticed, all the time.

"I don't need the drink," Kevin said, "but I'll say hi. If you change your mind about the parade-"

"I won't."

"But if you do, shoot me a message. You're on my media."

"Have a great day," Ben said, turning around and walking briskly back into the office. He could feel Kevin's eyes on him until the door closed.

Minutes later, the door opened, and Bobby re-entered. "He likes you," Bobby said.

"You're out of line."

"He's a good guy, Ben. And certainly good looking. I just want you to see you happy again. We all do."

"We?"

"The whole team. Tiny says Kevin always asks if you're in when he shows up."

"I'm not looking for a boyfriend," Ben said.

"Just a friend then."

"I don't need any of those either. Have a good night, Bobby."

Ben sat down at his desk and started pushing paper around, hoping Bobby would take the hint. Still, he could see Bobby out of the corner of his eye, looking down at him. "And I don't need your pity either, Bobby. Now, good night."

"Happy Pride, boss," Bobby said.

"Meh" was Ben's only reply.

Bobby left then, and Ben sat there staring at a computer screen that wasn't even on, knowing he should go home but not able to make himself move. After a while, he lay down on the couch and closed his eyes.

Sometime after that, he opened his eyes, and we have seen what he saw: the still strangely sexy specter of his long dead lover. When he opened his eyes after that, it was not Jake standing over him though.

What he saw this time was someone wholly different in every way. Jake was what the kids now called masc; there was no denying he was a man. This new person still appeared somewhat masculine but was dressed in a flowing pink gown. Her lips were painted red, and her smile was wide. Still though, as wide as the smile was, her eyes – deep and dark – were hauntingly sad. It wasn't really apparent if she was just a queen or if she was trans, but she was beautiful and familiar, dark-skinned and lithe of limb, with a crown of flowers upon her black curls: roses and tulips mostly, with baby's breath falling down across her forehead.

"Who are you?" Ben asked, sitting upright. He couldn't remember falling asleep – and refused to even entertain the notion that he had cried himself to sleep. The clock on wall showed 9:00 in bright red letters, but whether AM or PM, he couldn't tell. "I feel I should know you. Have we met?"

"We haven't, until now," she said, her voice manly and deep and yet still not out of place with her feminine-presenting dress and look. "I am the Ghost of Pride Past. I had another name, when I walked among you, when I threw bricks and raised hell, but now, I am simply what you see: a spirit proud of what has come before." She paused, looking at Ben, and then rolling her eyes and sighing. "Oh. Of course. You probably think I'm *her*. I'm not. I knew her, of course. She was great, too great. The rest of us got lost in her shadow sometime. People thought it was funny we had the same name. The *other* Marsha, they called me."

"What do you want with me? Nothing you say will make me go to the parade tomorrow, and frankly, I don't understand why the spirit world cares one way or another if I go. Why can't I see Jake again?"

"His spirit cannot show you what you need to see, but trust me when I say, you will see him. I will take you to him now, if you'd like."

"I would like to sleep, is what I would like. It's a busy weekend, and I do not have time to spend chatting with ghosts or spirits or whatever you all are. Still, you say

I could see him? He said, when he was here before, that he didn't think that could happen. He left so quickly…"

"The spirit that visited you was right. You will not see each other again this night. But still, if you come with me now, you will see Jake again."

"If, you say? You mean, I have a choice?"

"Consent is crucial," the spirit said. "Other times, before, we didn't worry so much, but now we know better. You can lead a horse to water, but you cannot make him drink, or think, after all. If you are not willing to learn, we will not force you."

"What happens if I say no?"

"I will go, and you will go on as you have been."

"And if I go? Things will be different?"

"That, I cannot say. That, I cannot see. I am of the past, Ben."

"Where do you want to take me?"

"Nowhere you have not been before," she said. She held out her hand. "Take my hand if you wish to come. In this, as in all things, the choice is yours."

"Take your hand? I can touch you? But aren't you a ghost?" He stood up but didn't reach out. "Jake had a glow about him. I don't see that with you."

"Some glow on the outside, for all to see. Some glow in a way that is more muted. Look closely though, Ben. You will see my glow."

He looked at her then, straight into her eyes. He saw a fire there, deep within. He could feel that fire - it burned hot, but it did not harm. It felt cleansing.

"I'm scared," he said.

"Change is scary," she said, nodding. "But you must decide quickly. Take my hand or sit back down. What is scarier though? That you will change, or that you won't?"

He did not want to change. Things were fine the way they were. His life was comfortable and familiar, and why then was there something inside him now, a spark – was it from her fire? Had she left something in him already? – a spark that flickered, and an ache that needed something else.

He took her hand.

Without moving, they had moved. Gone was his office, its flickering fluorescents, brick walls, and messy desks (yes, desks, Jake's desk was still there, and just provided another surface to pile up with cash outs and receipts and contracts and advertisements and all the other paper that accumulated).

Instead, they were suddenly on a busy sidewalk. Like, packed busy. The sun was high and hot, and the sky was an incredible shade of blue, what sky he could see anyway. Buildings towered overhead, and Ben knew this skyline.

"Calgary," he said. "Why are we here?"

"When are we, here, should be your question," she said. "It's June 1994 and look across the street."

He followed her pointed finger and saw himself, twenty years younger. Oh, he was gangly, with brown bangs flopping across a forehead still plagued by adolescent acne. He knew what this was now, and he told her. "My first time at a pride parade."

She nodded, and as if in response, the parade began to come down the street. Ben knew what was going to happen, and Ben was watching for him. There he came, at the very front of the parade: tall, dark, and handsome, waving the rainbow flag with such passion. Ben looked at his younger self watching him with lust and admiration and excitement.

It was a queer youth group leading the parade, and this William was a part of it. As he marched, getting closer to Young Ben, he was inviting other teens who were lining the street watching to join in. Most didn't, but some did. And then they got to Young Ben, and William waved at him to join them.

Young Ben looked at William, standing there, so beautiful. Ben had certainly seen hot guys before, but… was it the way his dark green eyes contrasted with the black of his hair? Was it the skin so perfectly tanned unlike Ben's own? This man was beautiful and proud, and in waving towards Ben, it was like he was saying "come, leave behind the closet and the cowardice and you can have all of this. You can have me."

Young Ben went running out into the street, and another member of the group handed him another flag. Right up front with William, Young Ben waved that flag with as much zeal as he did, at first a step behind, so he could mimic William's movements, and then he stepped forward, marching side by side. William turned and introduced himself, and somehow, Young Ben found the speech to do the same. William flashed a devastatingly perfect smile; Young Ben fell in love.

"Look at you there," the other Marsha said. "The very front of a parade, and now, you won't even go watch one."

"It was different then," Ben said. "The whole world was different."

"I know how the world can change," she said, with a knowing smile. "What did this day mean to you though?"

The noise of the parade faded, as if she had turned down the volume on the memory (or the time travel or the dream or whatever it was). He was in his past with a transgender ghost; now was not the time for questioning things.

"I had only been out for a couple years," Ben said, "and I felt so free finally being able to express who I was. I wanted the whole world to know, and I didn't care if they cared. This was the perfect way. My mom saw me on the news, you know. She asked if I was going to become one of those kind of gays – the political in your face ones, I guess she meant. It was something she always preferred to ignore about me." He paused, remembering the weird mixture of concern and fear and distaste that his mother wore whenever the topic of Ben's sexuality was raised. "Until Jake anyway," he went on. "Then she didn't really have a choice. She had to accept him, because he was my everything." It was more than he had meant to admit, to this spirit who already knew too much.

Ben watched Young Ben get lost in the sea of people. He hadn't thought of William in years. He was so beautiful, but Ben knew how this would end. After the parade, William would invite Ben for drinks with his friends, and those drinks with friends would become drinks just the two of them, and that would become William asking Ben to come over. Young Ben wouldn't be able to believe he was in bed with this paragon of physical perfection; next to him, in bed, he would feel as if every thing he hated about his own body was highlighted and amplified. Until William's vodka-soaked kisses would drive away all thought entirely, and then they would sleep and then…

"What happened the next morning?"

"You can read my mind?"

"Of course, Ben. Still, it works best if you tell me."

"I don't think I realized just how much William drank that night. He was so hungover, and he basically just kicked me out. Don't get me wrong; it was hardly my first one-night stand. I just thought maybe, he was different. Hungover, he certainly wasn't the charismatic guy leading that parade." Ben paused. He hadn't thought about William in years, but now that he was, he realized a question had always lingered. "So, you know the past, right?

She nodded.

"What happened to him after that? I saw him a couple times. He was always hammered, and I don't think he remembered me."

"His story isn't mine to tell you, Ben."

"Oh, come on," Ben said. "After all, I came back here with you. I had to see that god-awful shirt I was wearing. I've never been a fashion gay, but what was I thinking? His story and mine overlapped, for that one night anyway. Can't you just tell me if he kept on kicking guys out of his bed and his life?"

"William died," she said. "Six years after this parade." Her voice was flat and cold. Maybe ghosts didn't care if they broke news gently.

Ben wasn't surprised though. He felt he had known this. He still had to ask. "How?"

"He drank himself to death."

Just what he figured. Loneliness. Ben looked at the parade as it passed by, the crowds on the sidewalk falling onto its tail to follow it to its beer gardens. "What now? Was that all this was about? To show me a time I was excited to be a part of Pride? I knew that. That wasn't a big reveal for me."

"All? Oh no, Ben. That's not even close." She held out her hand, and sighing, Ben took it.

The dance mixes of that early 90s Pride parade gave way to the fast-paced techno house of a turn of the millennium gay club. Ben knew this place – of course he did. He was there every day. It was Good Judy's, and he turned to see himself behind the bar.

"I remember those highlights in my hair," he said. "What was I thinking? And ugh, this music. It's particularly vile after just hearing those great tracks."

The other Marsha smiled at Ben, and said, "child, you don't even know good gay club music unless you came of age and came out on the disco round. But you know where we are?" Ben nodded. "Do you know *when*?"

He looked around, and then he knew. He watched himself get introduced to Jake, a recent hire, temporary anyway, just for pride weekend. Ben was to show him the ropes and help him along, and any annoyance Ben felt at being saddled with a novice on the busiest nights of the year simply melted away when he looked into Jake's eyes.

Even now, looking at Young Ben look at Younger Jake, Ben felt his heart beat faster.

"Busy hey?" were Jake's first words to him, and Ben remembered the disappointment at thinking the pretty face was covering a stupid mind. Of course it was busy. It had been a year before Ben told Jake about that reaction, to which Jake confessed that it was a stupid thing to say, and it only came out of his mouth because he was as immediately stricken with infatuation as was Ben.

Things began to move even faster than they had that night, like the Spirit was running everything at a slightly faster speed. The crowds came and drank and danced, and the bar was filled with the shirtless and the beautiful and the people who only come out that one weekend a year. Ben hardly noticed any of that though. While he poured drink after drink after drink, his eyes kept drifting to the novice – the novice who had lost his shirt and stood there now as bare-chested and glistening as anyone on that dance floor.

Then the scene dissolved around them (what? No star wipe? Ben asked her), and he and Jake were sitting at Ashley's. Ashley's was the 24-hour diner where all the staff from all the clubs all went when the bars closed and the lights came on and customers were gone home to pass out. The rest of the Good Judy's team had passed on Ashley's (honestly, it was becoming less of a tradition. The food had been much better with the old owner, back when it was still Mary Kate's). Ben and Jake sat there at the table, splitting cheese fries and chicken strips and cup after cup of coffee, and suddenly they looked around to notice the bar staff were all long gone, and there was daylight streaming through the window.

"Morning already," Jake said. Another less-than-stellar observation from a more-than-pretty face, Ben thought.

"We should get out of here," Ben said. "Get some sleep before the parade and before it all starts up again."

Jake nodded, and they paid their bill and walked out into the fresh morning air. Through the buildings, the sky was pink, the morning sun reflecting off the glass of the towers all around them. Ben found himself taking Jake's hand. Jake looked down, and smiled, and did not take it away.

"I really do need to get some sleep though," Ben said. "But…"

"But?"

"You could probably sleep over. Get a few hours, hit the parade? Then nap before work?"

"Or something before work," Jake said, squeezing Ben's hand. "And I'd love to."

Ben turned to the other Marsha. "Why? Why this scene? Do you ever think I could have forgotten the night we met? Have you forgotten the night you met anyone you loved?"

"Sometimes," she said, "not forgetting isn't the same as remembering. It was pride that brought you together, pride that led you to you love…"

"And so? Jake is dead. Nothing I remember will change that. Me celebrating pride won't change that. What good does it do to show me this night?"

"What good may come is for someone else to show and say. Like I said, Ben, I am of the past."

"So, is there more then? Or are you done with me? How many past prides are we revisiting? Busy nights, drunken nights, high nights, magic nights, chaotic nights, yes I get it."

"Do you though?" She held out her hand.

The sun was hot outside, and Ben was on a float next to himself. A disconcerting experience to say the least, but Ben was, for lack of a better way proud how he was handling things. Part of him knew he was likely just having far too vivid dreams caused by anxiety over the busy weekend, and that soon, he would wake up in his office and all would be fine, but part of him –

“You don’t believe?” she said.

“You’re showing me nothing I haven’t already lived through. What will I possibly gain or learn from seeing the same thing twice?”

“In other words,” she said, “show you something you don’t know?”

“Yes.”

She grabbed him by the hand and the float and the sun dissolved and suddenly, he was somewhere else. It was a dark bar, and he did not know it. It was small and crowded, and everywhere, men talked quietly in corners. At a table in front of him sat a black man, who looked somewhat familiar.

“Is that you?” Ben said.

“That was how I was born,” she said. “This is who I am.”

“This is your past then? Your past pride?”

“This is before pride. There were no parades yet, no celebrations. There wasn’t any rainbow flag hanging outside to let people know ‘we’re here, we’re queer’. Hell, there wasn’t even a rainbow flag yet. And yet....”

“And yet what?”

“Watch.”

Ben watched the man peer over the glass of draught beer he was drinking. His eyes followed another man around the bar, a man in moss green pants that sat too high. This, with a shirt that was orange and yellow plaid. Ben couldn’t see the attraction but could clearly tell, there was attraction there. Attraction and fear.

"Is this seat taken?" Moss Pants said.

"No, please, sit."

Moss Pants sat down but Marsha's ghost just stared into his beer. Marsha's ghost, Ben though. The ghost of a ghost. Maybe he wasn't handling this as well as he thought he was. What was the name of this man in front of him? Whatever it was, it was a dead name – dead, ghosts, perfect, his interior monologue went.

Moss Pants smiled. "I haven't seen you in here before," he said.

"I just moved here," Marsha's ghost said without looking up.

'You're very attractive," Moss Pants said, and Marsha's ghost blushed and gulped his beer.

"I'd never had a man say that to me before," she said. "This was my first week in New York. I didn't even know why I had moved there. I just knew it was where I had to be. It was long before I started to cross dress, and long before my sex change. I hadn't even heard of a sex change back then. I just knew that when this man said he wanted to be with me, I wanted to be with him."

"Did you go home with him?"

"Oh yes, I went home with him and we fell madly in love and we were together forever, and it was a happy gay ever after. Watch."

Moss Pants had his hand on Ghost's Ghost's knee. Ben could see how nervous and excited and terrified he was. They finished their drinks, and they stood up, and Moss Pants led the way to the back of the building, where they exited through a back door.

"Ready to see my happy ending?" the spirit said, indicating Ben should follow.

They walked through the bar, through the people even, and out into the alley, where Moss Pants had him pinned down to the ground. Out of the shadows of the alley stepped another man, two men, three men.

This was not a fairy tale.

"Sick faggot."

"Fucking queer."

The figure on the ground barely made a noise as they kicked him and punched him and spit on him, and just before the figure blacked out entirely, they rolled him onto his stomach, and ripped his pants down, and…

The scene faded, and they were back standing in Good Judy's. Ben looked at the spirit standing next to him; down her cheeks rolled tears made black with eye-liner.

"They knew what I was before I did," she said, after a moment. "And they hated me. But I did not hide. Oh no, I learned to fight back. I came out as a gay man, and then came out again as a transsexual woman, and all the time, I fought back against people who hated me."

"I'm sorry you went through that. Thank you," Ben said, "thank you for sharing that with me." There was a pain in his chest. Suddenly, his own losses seemed smaller.

"It isn't about comparing pain," she said. "Everybody hurts in their own way. I showed you that so you would listen to me when I tell you that you have a choice coming."

"Can I ask you something?"

"Ask away."

"Before, you said you got a happy ending – "

"Sarcasm clearly."

"But did you ever get one? After that?"

She paused. It was a pause pregnant with meaning. Ben couldn't read thoughts like this ghost before him could, but he could read that pause. It was a pause that contained all the memories of all the years this ghost had lived, before whatever had happened to make her this shade in front of him. "Your turn first, Benjamin." She grabbed his hand.

The sun was high and hot, and he was on a float next to himself. Next to other him, Jake stood, shirtless and waving as the float went by the screaming crowds. The bar was theirs now, Ben knew; this was their first parade. It was even more special because it really was like everything had come together. They were happy. They had built a dream together. Good Judy's was the number one spot in town.

The float was filled with people he had known: staff that had worked for him, many of whom had gone on to other things; customers he had known, many of whom had gone on to other places. Each one warmed his heart to see.

There was Billy, a decade younger, his hair bleached blond and streaked with purple (had THAT ever been a good look?). There was Tina, towering over everyone on the float, a massive bull dyke / head of security, long before she became a drag king under the ironic name Tiny. Billy and Tina were the only people on this float that were still at the club.

People left. Ben knew that. Even before Jake left, even before Jake died, Ben knew that. Leaving was just what people did. Josh and Mario had married and moved to the coast. Dallas had moved to the coast as well, but last Ben had heard, he was methed-out. Markus hadn't managed to move before he'd overdosed, choking to death on his own vomit. Lisa and Lucy lived in the suburbs, two kids, two dogs, two cats, too perfect. People left.

He remembered then, standing in that memory as he was, he remembered remembering in that moment a time from years before, when he had just come out to his mother, and how she looked at him with tears in her eyes – eyes the same brown as his own - and told him she still loved him, but oh, it was just such a lonely life, and she was worried for him. There, at that moment, on that magic float in that incredible parade surrounded by amazing people, Ben had known she was wrong. It wasn't a lonely life; it was a wonderful one.

"Do you still feel that?" she said.

"No," he said honestly. "Mom was right. It's a lonely life."

"Were you lonely here?"

"No," he admitted.

"But every moment after this? You were lonely for all of them?"

"Not all, no. But many." He felt a wave of grief flooding over him, like it had the night Jake died. "So many."

"We all feel grief, Benjamin. We all feel lonely."

"I've never said that isn't true," Ben said, as the parade passed by hundreds of people cheering in the street and the sounds of disco divas and pop queens mingled in the air. Everywhere, rainbows flew. "Look, don't make it seem like I've tried to claim some ownership of loneliness. I haven't. I know other people are just as miserable, more so even. But…."

"But what?"

"It just got too hard," he said. "If there was a way to bottle what I felt this day, the way the sun stayed out for the whole parade, the way everyone was there and they all mattered to me, the way there were no protestors claiming we were all going to hell – for the first time ever, mind you – it was just a perfect day, and if it could have been bottled up, I could have lived off it forever, but that can't happen. Soon, that feeling fades away, and people leave, and people change, and people die, and everything just becomes so unbelievably fucking hard…"

"I know hard, Ben." She held out her hand again. "Here, come."

Gone were the crowds, again. They stood in a hospital room, and it wasn't one Ben knew. Ben had certainly seen his share of hospital rooms – from the one where his mom passed away from the cancer that had spread so fast through her, to the one where Markus had been time and time again before finally dying at home alone. Now, though, on the bed in front of him was the shell of a man, sunken and gray. Holding his hand, wearing the same floral crown, was a slightly younger version of the ghost next to him.

"I met Charles in 1976," she told Ben.

"I've known you for ten years," the younger her said to the man in the bed.

"We had a wonderful life," she told Ben.

"We had a wonderful life," she said to the man in the bed.

"Even now, in those last months, he could make me laugh like no one else."

"You can always make me laugh. How will I laugh without you?"

"I didn't have to worry though," she said to Ben. "Not long after Charles died, I got sick. I faded fast. Like I couldn't bear to be in the world without him."

"I don't know how to live in the world without you."

Charles opened his eyes. "You will live though," he said, in slightly accented English. "You are so strong." Each word was a labor. "*Mi hermosa flor*."

Ben looked at the spirit next to him, his eyebrow raised.

"My beautiful flower," she translated. She turned back to the bed, where Charles' eyes were closed now. "He doesn't ever open them again."

"I'm sorry," Ben said. "But why show me this? I mean, thank you for sharing this, but why? It must be hard to relive it."

"Hard? No. Wonderful. To see him again? Even like this? What was hard was living through it. Can you imagine the guilt, that I had been the one who infected him? Can you imagine the anger, that he may have been the one who infected me? Can you imagine the grief, as I watched him fade, and still seemed to bloom, his beautiful flower?"

"I can't," Ben said. "I can't even imagine it." Jake had been there one minute and gone the next. This – wasting away... it was something else entirely.

"But we had those ten years," she said. "And they were wonderful. This moment though? This scene?" She watched herself sitting there. "This was one of the worst moments of my life." She sniffed back a tear and reached out to grab Ben's hand. As the scene faded away, Ben heard the solid beep of the flatlining ECG.

They were back at Good Judy's, back in his office, but it was different. It was like a cyclone had been trapped within the walls. Papers were everywhere. Pictures were smashed. Jake's desk lay on its side.

Ben knew this night.

He – well, the slightly younger he – stormed in through the door, looking frantically about. "There must be something else I can smash!" He slammed the door behind him.

It opened back up almost immediately. Bobby and Tiny rushed in. “We're sorry, boss. We thought you would want us to go ahead with business like normal this weekend.”

“Nothing is normal!” Ben yelled. “Nothing has been normal since --” He looked at Jake's empty chair, laying on its side, and he collapsed onto the couch.

“Look, boss,” Bobby said, “we know things are different now, but it's pride weekend. We had to enter a float into the parade. The staff expect it. A gay bar can’t not participate in pride. The community expects it!”

“Meh! I don't care! Community? Fuck the community! There isn’t any community.” Ben was wrong, of course. We know it, and you know it. There is a community, and it’s an important one, a vibrant one, an eternal one. It’s not one you simply become part of by identifying as one of those letters in the ever-growing acronym – oh no, it’s more than that. It’s all the individuals and groups and businesses that are committed to making real their vision of a world where gender identity and sexual orientation aren’t factors in how we relate to each other as human beings. If you don’t have that end game in mind, you may be a G or an L or a B or a T, but you’re missing a big point.

None of that mattered though, in Ben’s rage as he went on. “How dare you? You should have asked! You should have told me! I shouldn't have found out when a fully decorated trailer pulls up outside my bar the night before.”

"We thought this would be easiest this year," Tiny said. "We thought this was what you and Jake would have wanted us to do."

"What Jake would have wanted," Ben said, turning to the other Marsha. "If I had a dollar for every time someone said that to me those first six months... You must eat. It's what Jake would have wanted. You need sleep. It's what Jake would have wanted. Apparently, all Jake wanted was to crash his car. All Jake wanted was to leave."

Ben watched himself cry on the couch. Bobby and Tiny stood there, in the doorway, clearly unsure what to do. They looked at each other and quietly stepped back, closing the door behind them and leaving Ben alone with his grief.

All Jake had wanted to do was leave Ben.

"Is that all he wanted earlier tonight?" she said. "Did he come here, back to this plane, wearing all those chains, because he wanted to leave you?"

"I don't know why he came. I don't know why you came. I don't know why any of this is even happening. I don't want to be anywhere you've taken me, especially not back here, feeling all of… this." He waved his hand at the mess in the office, and the crying mess of his broken, former self.

"Who is the one who wants to leave then?" she said.

"So what if I do?" Ben screamed, even as Ben-on-the-couch cried. "So what if I want to leave? No one will care."

The clock struck nine and the office faded away, to be replaced by... the office again. Ben sat up on the couch. Had he been sleeping? Dreaming? Regardless, it was true.

He had known for a long time that none of it – bar or community or Jake – none of it really mattered.

“And that's where I come in,” said the smooth-bodied blond muscle hunk in glittery gold booty shorts that suddenly appeared at the foot of the couch. “I'm the Ghost of Pride Present, but that's a bit of a mouthful.” Ben couldn't help but glance down, at what was also a mouthful. A very impressive mouthful. The ghost saw, and smirked. “You can call me Marc.”

“I'm done,” Ben said. “This whole nocturnal spiritual journey is over.”

“It's just beginning,” Marc said.

“It ends now. If I don't go, you can't make me.”

“Oh, that's her rule, not mine.” Marc reached down with a meaty hand and yanked Ben off the couch. “Besides, there’s not a gay man alive or dead who doesn’t want to come with me. Happy Pride!” Marc said, and he kissed Ben on the cheek.

So. Many. Lesbians.

That was Ben's first impression.

They were in an apartment and it was overflowing with lesbians. Ben knew he shouldn't assume orientation, but the combination of rainbow flags, leather, and plaid was a giveaway. No one in the room had hair longer than her shoulders. It was a great big lesbian stereotype party.

Some may have been bisexual. We shouldn’t participate in the erasure that has so often happened to our bi brothers and sisters. Some could have been pansexual. Some could have been straight, even. We shouldn't be making a judgment of orientation based on appearance, but it was Pride morning, and for one moment, we can pretend that all the Ls and Bs and Ts (and Ps and As and even the heterosexuals) will understand our intent wasn't to offend.

"What do you call a group of lesbians?" Marc said.

"What?"

"A group of lesbians. Like a murder of crows or a gaggle of geese."

"I have no idea."

"A U-Haul!"

Ben rolled his eyes. "It's a good thing they can't hear you," he said, "or it won't be crows getting murdered." He paused. "Where am I, and who are these people?"

"Watch," Marc said, throwing his arm around Ben's shoulders. Clearly, he was some sort of gym-bro gay, and was it even possible for ghosts to have sex, Ben suddenly wondered, because this ghost was hot!

The door to the apartment opened and in came Tiny, followed by her girlfriend, Sara. Tiny was in drag, of course, wearing her signature rainbow tuxedo, her hair slicked back, her fake beard attached. Sara, by contrast, was in a white wedding dress.

"Never fear, ladies, we have arrived!"

"About time, Tiny!" one called out. "We have to leave in twenty minutes."

"Stop your queefing!" She set a bottle of champagne on the counter. "Let's get this poured then. Can't let the gays have all the mimosa fun!"

Sara slapped her playfully. “Stop saying that 'queefing' thing. It's foul!”

Tiny grabbed her and pulled her in for a kiss. “That why you love me, wife,” she said, licking Sara's face. Lesbians laughed everywhere, as champagne got popped and poured.

“Happy Pride!” they cheers'd.

“Now,” Tiny said, “who's coming on our float? We have lots of room.” Five or six raised their hands. “That's it? C'mon, ladies. We cannot let the men overpower us again this year. You know Bobby would have the float all twinks if he could.”

“Yes, come on,” Sara said. “We don't have a lesbian bar anymore, not since Lix closed. We have to show support for the spaces that support us.”

“It's true,” Ben told Marc. “I would love to see more lesbian support. That's why all their spaces close. I've seen so many dyke bars close in the last two decades, just from lack of support.”

“But you don't care about pride,” Marc said slyly.

“Pride! Meh! I mean, in general. In between nesting. The lesbians can't all go drinking at straight sports bars.”

“Why not?” Marc asked. “After all, it's 2018, right? Everywhere is gay-friendly now.”

“That's not true.”

“Of course it is. That's been the goal all along, right? No need for gay pride, no need for gay bars. Then you can retire and be done with it all.”

Is that what Ben wanted? Surely not. He had been doing it so long, and yes, he had seen times change from a dozen local gay bars, to just the one. He had seen rights marched for, and attained. He had seen the protesters dwindle and practically disappear.

Was there really a need for Good Judy's anymore? Was there a need for him?

There was a knock at the door. Tiny opened it. "Look, it's Cynthia! I didn't think you'd come."

At the door was a girl. She didn't even look twenty.

"Come in, come in," Tiny said, towering over the short newcomer. "Everyone, this is Cynthia. She was at the club last night. She's brand new!"

The other women welcomed her – and did so much less appraisingly than a group of guys probably would have done, had a new pretty face walked into the room, Ben noted.

"This is her first ever pride," Tiny said. "I told her we'd keep her safe."

Sara offered Cynthia a mimosa.

"Are you going on the GJ's float?"

"Oh, I --"

"C'mon, no point being shy," Tiny said. "You've done the hard part. You came out. You set foot in a queer bar. Hell, you came here! What's one more step?"

"Well, maybe," she said. "It would be kinda cool."

"One more!" Tiny said, and they cheers'd again. "Bobby has his work cut out for him this year. Now quick, ladies, let's get you dykes to your bikes, and the rest of us to the float. It's parade time!" Tiny finished off her mimosa in one gulp.

Marc leaned over and kissed Ben on the cheek again.

Going from mimosa-drinking lesbians to *this* was culture shock. Ben found himself standing among a bevy of shirtless gays, taking turns smearing rainbows over their sculpted abs.

"This is what I call Pride," Marc said, looking around appreciatively. "Doesn't this do anything for you at all?"

Ben looked around. Every body could have been screenshotted from an app, so flawless they must have been Photoshopped or at least filtered, but they were real. There, a thin dusting of perfectly cropped hair covering mocha choca latte pectorals. There, a bubble butt; there, a bulging bicep. "They're hot, but so what? There are hot men through the door every day. That's nothing to be proud of. Their bodies will eventually conspire against them, if they don't drink or drug or fuck themselves to death first."

"Damn, you're dark! What made you like this?"

"Wait what? You don't know?"

"Ghost of Pride Present," he said, pointing at himself. "Remember? I don't get the backstory. I just live in the moment."

"A stupid way to live," Ben said. "How can you plan for tomorrow?"

"Your way is better? You're busy planning for tomorrow? That's what you're doing, sitting there in your office all by yourself?"

"I'm keeping busy. I'm paying bills. I'm getting by." He looked around. He knew these guys, from the club. Maybe not their names, but their stories. They were pretty. They were wanted. They thought they had it all, and right now, they did. Had he ever been that young?"

"Like I said, I don't get the backstory. Were you ever that young?"

"You have the mind-reading down though."

"I'll tell you this. It's written all over your face."

Ben turned to face Marc. "What is?"

"When you're not obsessing about the future, you're obsessing about the past. That's no way to live, Ben."

"You don't know what I've gone through -"

"Doesn't matter. Shhhh. Watch." Marc clamped his hand over Ben's mouth.

"Okay, boys, how are we doing?" Bobby came waltzing into the room, carrying a tray of shots. "Fireball breakfast!"

Fireball, is of course, not something we would ever recommend for breakfast. None of your national food guides list cinnamon flavoured alcohol as an acceptable meal substitute; the lesbians had trays of vegetables they'd devoured before our visit. Gays, on the other hand, had one rule on the morning of the parade: eat nothing that will distort abs. One didn't devote six months to cardio and core and crunches just to undo it at the last moment by consuming a heavy carb breakfast.

"Happy pride," they cheers'd.

Ben knew these boys. Some were staff – whom he greeted nightly and then ignored as best he could, content to let Bobby handle the details. Some were customers – whom he would greet each night, with a handshake or a hug or a shot before twirling onto the next and the next and the next as he spun back in the safety of his office.

Thomas with the curls. Ryan with his perfect scruff. Doug with the dreamy eyes and his boyfriend Alex, the insanely talented photographer. Brayden and Josh and Dan and Eric and a whole bunch more he didn't have names for and just called "handsome" or "babe" or "hey stranger" as he wove amongst them night after night.

There was no specific type – they were blond and brunet and dark; they were barely old enough to drink and seasoned party professionals; there were hairless twinks and muscled otters and furry bears. Yes, Bobby had organized it so there were definitely more of the hairless twink variety. Some looked so young, Ben though, and that made Ben feel so old.

"But they all have something in common too," Marc said. "They are proud."

"Hey, I'm proud!"

"Are you?"

"Yes! Just because I don't want to be in a parade with a bunch of kids still excited that they take it up the ass doesn't mean I'm not proud." Ben paused. "Okay, that sounded harsh even to me." Marc smiled, and when he smiled, his dimples flared, and when his dimples flared, Ben melted at the knees.

Ben looked around. They stood there, invisible, amongst this room of celebrating gays. Invisible like those bisexuals that so often got erased. These men didn't look alike at all. There really wasn't much in common other than a love for dick and…

"They all look so happy," he said suddenly. Physically, they were all different, but they were all smiling, and more, their eyes all… were so alive. It wasn't just happiness in those eyes; it was excitement and hope and… real pride

Marc took Ben by the arm and spun him around to face a mirror. In the mirror, Ben saw the pre-parade party disappear. It was just him and Marc (who truly was a sculpted god – do ghosts lift? Ben flashed to an image of Casper crossfitting).

"You're supposed to be looking at yourself," Marc said. "Besides, you aren't interested in guys right now."

Ben looked at himself. His eyes carried so much baggage under them, and inside, they were... flat.

"Your eyes are deader than mine," Marc said, "and I'm a ghost."

"How did you die?" Ben asked.

"I'm actually not that kind of ghost. Past, she was real. Me? I'm just the spectral incarnation of the spirit of the times. Plus, you know, I'm hot, so that doesn't hurt." He smirked. "C'mon, Benjamin, let's get a move on. Pride may be eternal, but a parade doesn't last forever."

He squeezed Ben's ass and they vanished into the ether again.

Ben heard the parade before he saw it. Tens of thousands of people lined the streets. Rainbows were everywhere: in the hands of small kids running and laughing, on the windows of the businesses nearby, heck, even wrapped around people's dogs.

The excitement was deafening, and then, it rose in a roar as ahead, the parade turned the corner. The first group was the Two-Spirit Association, marshalling this year's parade in a way of elevating the queer, indigenous population and recognizing that the parade took place on Treaty land. There was a dignity about the headdresses worn by the elders that marched first. Ben knew them; there had been a 2S event at the Good Judy's earlier in the year. These were real headdresses, not colorful Village People-esque ones; Ben had had a very lengthy conversation with one of those elders about appropriation versus appreciation, and they had had to agree to disagree (Ben just couldn't come around to it ever being okay to wear a headdress of any kind)

The local chapter of PFLAGT came next. It was sure a far cry from Ben's first parade, which had seen four parents marching proudly. This group was huge, and not just mothers. Ben knew the chapter president; her name was Gladys and she was a grandmother of three lesbians. Ben knew the granddaughters too; one, Colleen, worked with a queer homelessness project that often hosted fundraisers at GJs. Colleen and her partner had just adopted a teenage daughter, one more thing for eighty-seven-year-old Gladys to be proud of.

Good Judy's itself was next, and Ben couldn't help but smile a little. The multi-leveled platform looked great. All the people he had just seen celebrating were gathered on it, intermingled. Tiny and Bobby played up the rivalry of the sexes, but when it came down to it, they were all together.

Bobby and Tiny were themselves on the top levels (the float looked like two pyramids, each pyramid six small levels - in rainbow colors, of course). Tiny was fist pumping the air, getting the crowd going, and Bobby was completely lost in the music, his hands folded at his chest almost as if in prayer and a huge grin plastered on his face as the DJ played one pride anthem after another.

"Old music!" Marc said. "Why didn't you just go with some good thump thump thump house? You know, music to fuck by?" He gyrated his hips to make his point clear. In those booty shorts, it was obvious he would make either a top or a bottom very happy.

"Because!" Ben said. "These songs, they're classic. They're more than classic. They capture the essence of what this is all about. They're about empowerment! They're about freedom! They're about our right to love and to fuck and to be who we want!"

Marc held up a mirror to Ben's face. There, he saw a flicker in his eyes. "See?" Marc said. "That fire is still in you. Who knew it would just take me dissing some pop diva to bring it out?"

Ben pushed the mirror down (even Marc's forearm was solid!). He watched the float, watched Bobby sway, and Tiny jump, and all the queers of all the colours dance. They were his tribe.

"No," he said, shaking his head. "They were my tribe. They will go on without me, just like I…" He trailed off.

"Just like you went on without Jake?" Marc grabbed Ben by the shoulders and kissed him hard. "You're not dead, Ben," he said, as they faded again.

They didn't shift far. They were lost in the crowd of the same parade. There was the back of the Good Judy's float. Next came the swim team, in their choreographed speedo-clad synchronicity. Their underwear parties were a highlight of the year at GJs.

In fact, Ben thought as he looked, every entry was connected in some way to the club. He had worked with this people, these groups, over the years. Some, he had worked with back in the olden days, when he was just a bartender working for Old Lady Paull, before he sold them the bar. Some, he and Jake had invited into the club, because Old Lady Paull had had very strong ideas about who was allowed in his gay bar. Some, he had helped start. All, he knew.

"Feeling any pride yet?" Marc asked.

“Meh,” Ben said, immediately. “They would have found homes, without me, without us. There’s some incredible people out there in this community. I don’t deny that. People with talent and strength and such unbelievable compassion-”

“Would it kill you to admit that you’re one of them? That you’ve given lots? That you’ve made the world better for so many of these people?”

“You’re getting a little to ‘It’s a Wonderful Life’,” Ben said, “and that's the wrong story. This isn’t supposed to be showing me what the world would be like without me.”

“And it’s not,” Marc said. “That’s not why we’re here.”

Marc pointed. Ben followed the line from his finger. There, amongst the crowd, was Kevin. Blue-eyed Kevin with that amazing wavy hair. He was standing by himself, watching the parade pass by. He was beaming, but the radiance of his smile just made Ben angry.

“Oh no,” he said. “I get enough of this from Bobby and Tina. I don’t need any matchmaking from a go-go-ghost.”

“No need to stutter,” Marc said. “And I’m not matchmaking. Matchmaking is so Future. I’m just in the moment.”

“So, what am I supposed to learn from watching Kevin?”

“Not watch,” Marc said, putting his hand (his soft hand, how could a body that hard have hands this soft), over Ben’s mouth. “Just listen.”

The noise of the crowd was gone. The noise of the parade was gone. It was like watching a video that had been muted. Then Ben heard it, Kevin's voice, coming from all around them.

"Yaaaaasssss. The swim team looks great. They really outdid themselves. They're so good every year. I bet they win Best Float. I wish Good Judy's would win though. They were impressive too. Ben should be proud. Ben should be on it. It's too bad. I understand why he doesn't want to. It is pretty commercial, I guess. Still, it would've been great if he was here."

"What is this?" Ben said.

"His interior monologue. Shush. You're supposed to be listening."

"I get it," Kevin continued to think. "At least, I think I do. He probably has so many guys hitting on him. He's good looking and successful. They're probably constantly knocking on his door."

"True?" Marc asked.

"Far from it," Ben said. "Everyone thinks that, but it's not the case at all, and even if it were, I'm not looking for anything."

"Bobby says Ben says he isn't looking for anything," Kevin went on, "but maybe I just don't do it for him."

"Does he?" Marc asked.

"Look at him. He's beautiful."

"Then why not?"

"Why does it matter? My sex life, or more accurately, my lack of a sex life, should hardly be a concern to you spirit types."

"I don't even really know him," Kevin thought. "But that's it exactly. I know him enough to know I want to know him more. I wish he was here to enjoy this with me."

"We aren't concerned about your sex life," Marc said, "but sex is a part of life for most of us, and clearly from the way you've been checking my package out, you're still very much a sexual being, so why, Ben, why?"

"Who has the time?"

"You've got nothing but time."

"He's too young."

"Age is just a number."

"And in his case, a very small one."

"Oh, not that small," Marc said, leering at Kevin's crotch.

"That's not what I meant. Size doesn't matter, anyway."

"But age does?"

"Yes! We have nothing in common."

"Which you know how?"

"I just do."

"What's the real reason?"

"I already told you."

"It's not his age."

"It is."

"It's not your schedule."

"It is!"

"What is it really?"

"That's it. Those two things!"

"Ben, c'mon."

"Leave me alone. It doesn't matter. I'm fine being alone."

"Are you?"

"Yes."

"Are you?"

"Yes!"

"Are you?"

"No! I fucking hate it okay? I go home every night, alone, and I wake up every morning alone, and it's been that way for so long that I barely remember what it feels like to have another man in my bed."

"Then why not date this guy that wants to date you? Why not try? Why not? What's the worst that could happen?"

"He could leave me the same way Jake did!"

Suddenly, they were back in Ben's office. The clock read 9:00. "Happy Pride," Marc said, kissing Ben on the cheek before fading away.

Ben being single had nothing to do with him not wanting to celebrate Pride. Did it? Some of his best pride memories were when he was single: the parties and the men and the laughs and the men and one very drunken night that ended in some skinny dipping.

But then along had come Jake, and since that first Pride together, they had been a couple, and Pride as a couple was different than Pride as a young and single and ready to mingle gay man. Well, for them as a couple anyway. There were probably lots of couples who did the open thing, who went out to the parade and the parties and found a hot guy or two to take home and fuck senseless. Ben and Jake had never been that.

By the time Pride Day was over, even sex with each other was the farthest thing from their minds. They had gone home and passed out, happy to be done it for another year. It was a physically and emotionally taxing day.

Ben remembered his first Pride after Jake moved out. The bed had felt so empty. By the time Jake died, Ben was used to the empty bed. The Ghost of Pride Past sure hadn't shown him any of those ones, had she? The nights Ben collapsed exhausted into his bed, breaking down about his ability to do this on his own, without Jake as a partner, without Jake at all.

No, Ben thought, it wasn't because of Jake leaving or Jake dying that he hated Pride. It was just different now. This would be what? Twenty-some years of parades and rainbows? Every year, it got a little more diluted. Every year, there was more acceptance than the year before. He wasn't kidding when he said it was too commercial. What did all these banks and utilities and media have to do with being queer? The actual queer groups and businesses were being pushed out slowly, to make room for the corporations who funded the increasingly expensive spectacle of it all. It was literally a live-action commercial that simply targeted the rainbow: 'you're queer, we're here, buy our beer and phones and laundry detergent'. Pride had been mainstreamed, and that was good, but that meant that there was simply less need for it all.

Ben was ahead of the curve, really. Him not celebrating pride was just the first step to a world not celebrating pride. Soon enough, no one would need it because no one would care what someone's sexual orientation or gender identity were. It would stop mattering, and then there wouldn't need to be a parade.

There probably wouldn't need to be a gay bar either, come to think of it, and so maybe he should get ahead of that curve too. Close down Good Judy's and...

...and what, he thought? What would he do without this place? After all these years in gay nightlife, what was he apart from this bar? And what about the staff that relied on him? Bobby and Tiny and all the rest? Sure, they could find other jobs, at other clubs, or doing other things entirely, but this place still mattered to them. He had seen that, in the way they celebrated today.

But he would likely live to see a day where gay bars were obsolete. All the customers? They could almost go wherever already. They were tons of straight venues that marketed to the gays now – after all, all that disposable income had to go to someone right?

Look at the line-up of events for after the parade, he thought! Fully half of them were in places that didn't identify as queer bars (could he still say queer? He couldn't keep up). Gay-for-a-day wasn't good enough, but those were the places being lauded and applauded, for being so open, and fuck the places that spent all week, every week, all year, being queer.

The fight was exhausting. That's what it was about. That's why he didn't celebrate pride, because celebrating pride hadn't gotten him anywhere except here: bitter and alone.

"Meh," he said, and closed his eyes. Just for a second.

DONG! DONG! DONG!

He opened his eyes.

DONG! DONG!

He had a digital clock. What was making that sound?

DONG! DONG! DONG! DONG!

He was not in the office. He was... nowhere, really. He was standing on something solid, but what kind of ground, he couldn't tell, for mist rolled through. All he could see, in every direction, was this mist, thick and silvery.

"Hello?" he called out. "Third spirit? Let's get this over with. There's nothing you can show me."

Out of the mist emerged a... something. They were in a black robe, with no visible skin, but Ben wasn't frightened.

"Oh yes," he said, "no face, no words, that's you, right?"

"Nope!" said a voice that was neither masculine or feminine as two hands pulled back a hood. Where the face would have been was a flicker. Now, it was a black man.

Flicker. Now, an Asian woman. Flicker, now something else, undefined race, undefined gender, undefined age.

Ben felt a little nauseated. “Will this-” he waved at the spirit's face, “will this keep happening?”

“You'll adjust,” he/she/they said, and the voice now sounded like two voices, or was it three, overlapped and in perfect sync.

“What should I call you?” Ben asked, looking away.

“What's in a name?” they said. “We are what we are, and what we will be.”

“But if we're going to do this, I need to call you something.”

“Call me Avenir,” they said.

“Glad we have that settled. Look, Avenir,” Ben said, looking them in the face. Making eye contact with an entity whose face kept changing was challenging, to say the least. “I've been thinking. There's not really any point in us continuing tonight's little adventures. Your friends already made their point. I should get out there and live and enjoy myself, and blah blah blah yada yada yada, so, if you don't mind, you can just drop me back at the office.”

“Oh Ben, Ben, Ben, Ben, Ben,” they said. “You're right, you know. You've seen what was, and you've seen what is, and that's all we can really know.”

“And you, you're just going to show me what will happen if I don't celebrate pride, or get back on the dating horse, or whatever?”

“The others have it easy,” they said. “This is what happened. This is what is happening. There's nothing solid about where we are going. The future is, like me, fluid. A thousand choices every day change the pictures we will see. Your choices, Ben? They're barely a blip on the radar of time."

"You sure know how to make a guy feel important."

"We're not important, Ben. None of us."

Ben looked at them. "What exactly is this supposed to be teaching me?"

"Come."

It was Good Judy's but unlike any way Ben had ever seen it. The line-up snaked down the street, a street which was closed off with fencing, allowing the crowd inside to spill out into the street. Everywhere, people were celebrating. Above the entrance hung a giant rainbow flag, but along the fence, every so often, other flags flew in the light June breeze: the pink, blue, and purple of the bisexuals, the pink, blue, and white of the transgender flag, the browns of the bear flag, the darker colors of the leather flag, plus a dozen other flags Ben didn't recognize.

Music filled the street, classic songs Ben knew, songs of empowerment and freedom and survival. They were sung by straight artists, by out artists, by people whose lives were filled with their own struggles and successes, stories which resonated for the people who heard their music and adopted the songs as their own.

The combination of flags and anthems meant one thing: this was a future pride. Ben turned to Avenir. "When is this?"

"A not so distant future," they said. "Look at this crowd. It is all races and ages and genders and sexualities. It is diverse and inclusive, and it is here celebrating, at a place you built." Avenir pointed. "And look."

It was Ben, Older Future Ben. His hair had silvered (will silver? Will have silvered? How does one speak of oneself, while standing in some projected future?) but it still looked good. He looked good, he thought. He looked… happy.

"Welcome, everyone!" Future Ben said, his voice booming over the speakers. The scattered conversations stopped, and all those hundreds of people cheered. "Happy Pride!" They cheered even louder, a cheer so loud it echoed off the surrounding buildings.

"We are so glad you all came down to join us today. Who enjoyed the parade?" Again, the noise was deafening. "A beautiful day, a beautiful Pride, and what a beautiful crowd!"

"So what?" Ben asked Avenir. "So Pride keeps going, and some future me gets back into it. So what?"

"That's not what we are here to see," Avenir said. "Watch and wait."

Future Ben kept ramping up the crowd, each roar louder than the one before. The sun was high overhead, the breeze just enough to make the flags dance, and as the music started up again, and everyone returned to dancing, Ben looked at Future Ben stepping down from the podium and realized part of him wanted this future.

"I think..." he started to say, but Avenir cut him off, with a finger across their lips.

Ben followed Avenir's finger. Down the street, away from the colorful festivities, marched a group of people, in tan and white. The only color was on the red ballcaps they wore. From one sidewalk to the other, they were a line of clones. All white, all male.

And getting closer.

"Make America Straight Again," they were shouting, as they neared the fence. Now, the people inside had noticed them. Some called out, mocking them, swearing at them. Most were trying to ignore them. Future Ben turned up the music.

But now, they were right at the fence, their hands on it, shaking the chain link. "Straight is Great. God Made Straight."

"Fuck off," Future Ben screamed at them. "Don't make us call the police."

"Straight! Straight! Straight!" they chanted over and over. The music was stopped now. Everyone was watching the mob outside, a mob becoming ever more unruly. There were so many of them.

"What is this?" Ben asked Avenir.

"This is a Future," they explained. "Where Straight Pride is a rallying cry. And where the push back is very real, and very dangerous."

As Avenir said it, the fence came down, and the khaki-clad mob stormed over. Everywhere Ben looked was sudden violence, fists flying, kicks and punches, and the cheering turned to screams, and then a gun shot echoed, and the world went gray.

"What is that supposed to teach me?" Ben said. "I know there's hate. I know there's violence. I know it's getting worse. I see it on the news. I see it on social media. I see it everywhere."

"And how does that make you feel?" Avenir asked.

"How do you think? Scared as fuck. When that man walked into that gay club with a gun, that could have been here. It can happen anywhere."

"So you hide?"

"I don't hide," he said. "This is a gay bar. And will always be one. We will fly that flag no matter who tries to tear it down. We survived AIDS. We survived the closet, and dammit, we will survive that future, if that's what happens."

"Good," Avenir said. "There is fire in you yet. The other Marsha told me there was. Marc wasn't sure. I am glad to see it. Shall we continue?"

Ben nodded.

Ben is right, of course. Many of us didn't survive AIDS. Many of us didn't survive the closet. Many of us were rejected by family and friends, driven from our homes, into the streets. Some found solace in the bottle, some in the needle. Some never found solace at all but succumbed to self-harm. Some were beaten to death by strangers. One was left to hang on a fence and changed a nation. Some were gunned down in their sanctuary, but we still feel their spirits pulse. But Ben is right. As a community, we survived. And we shall continue.

They were in a courthouse. The gallery was filled with people waiting. There was a buzz in the air, excited, perhaps, or angry. Nervous for sure. Ben looked around. A statue of Justice stood in front of the bench, her eyes bound in rainbow cloth.

That was the first thing that was somewhat off.

The second thing was the person at the prosecution table. If she was a lawyer, she was certainly dressed differently than you'd see on television. Formal, still, yes, if a full length sequined gown counted as formal. She wore gloves though, which seemed the wrong kind of formal, and was that a tiara set into her mound of golden curls?

Ben was distracted by the bailiff shouting, "All Rise. The honorable Judge Tiny presiding."

Ben watched as Tiny – for it was indeed her – entered the courtroom and sat at the bench. The black robe flowed off her massive shoulders.

"Be seated all. We are here today to try this man-" she waved towards the defendant, a man so ordinary that Ben hadn't even noticed him sitting there, in his brown suit, with his flat hair - "Robert Johnson, for the crime of being normal. How do you plea?"

The man stood. "Not guilty, Your Honor."

Normal? Surely Ben must have misheard.

"Madam Prosecutor, you may begin."

The woman in the dress rose. “Thank you, your Honor.” Ben looked again. The sound of her voice left no doubt. This was a drag queen. Certainly, drag queens have been known to judge, but to practice law? This was different.

“This case is rather open and shut, your Honor. We really just need to speak to Mister Johnson.”

“Proceed.”

“Mister Johnson, do you deny that you're about as normal as they come?”

“Why, yes, yes I do.” His voice was timid, clearly frightened.

“But you admit that you're an accountant?”

“Yes, that's what I do. We all need accounting!”

“And you admit that your heritage is WHITE?”

“Well, I can't really deny my skin color.”

“And you're cisgender?”

The crowd gasped as the man nodded.

“Mister Johnson, how do you define your sexual orientation?”

“I don't see what that...”

“Answer the question, please.”

He mumbled.

“Your Honor, please instruct the defendant to speak up.”

“You heard the Queen. Speak up, Mister Johnson.”

“Heterosexual,” he said, the word stumbling out of his mouth, barely audible.

The crowd began to rumble, and suddenly, a group stood up in the back, chanting "Too late! We're straight! We don't want any more hate!"

"Bailiffs!" Judge Tiny yelled. "Clear this courtroom! Order! Order!"

"Robert Johnson," Judge Tiny said, "you have been found guilty. Not just of the crime of being normal but of the following more serious charges. As a cisgender, heterosexual, white male, you are responsible for the collective crimes of your ancestors and peers. You are responsible for centuries of discrimination and oppression. You are responsible for upholding the entrenched and systemic racism and misogyny and homophobia and transphobia that have caused such hurt to our disadvantaged. Your privilege has EXPIRED."

Ben turned to Avenir. "This cannot be at all possible."

"All things are possible. This? It's not likely." The courtroom faded away into fog. "But imagine a world where the pendulum swings so far the other way. Where straight people are persecuted simply for choosing to love members of another gender. Where people falsely identify as bi just so others think they may at least live a same-sex life. Where anything that mirrors a traditional gender role is scorned."

"We wouldn't ever let things get to that," Ben said.

"Well, certainly not you," Avenir said. "You have withdrawn from society, from the fight for a better society, a more just society. Wouldn't this future be better though? A future where the disadvantaged can begin to address millenia of discrimination. Would it really be so far off to think that, again, the oppressed could become the oppressors? We have seen it before. Don't you see it happening even now? Words are censored every day."

"But only because we have learned that words hurt," Ben said. "It isn't restrictive; it's corrective."

"Who are you to decide what is correct, and what isn't? Who made you judge, and jury, and social justice executioner? After all, that courtroom, it was built on the ashes of Good Judy's. Your bar became your funeral pyre. Whether it was self-inflicted arson was never found out."

"Look," Ben said. "That was a nice little break. Who doesn't enjoy some courtroom drama, but if all you have to share with me are visions of a future that would never come to pass, I have a club to open."

"Yes. Your club. Let's tune in on a future for your Good Judy's."

The fog rolled away. Ben knew the bar they stood in. He stood in it every day, and yet...this place was dingy! How had it got like this? The floor tiles were chipped. The stools around the tables had peeling upholstery. This was not his place.

He looked at Avenir. "I would never let this happen either," he said.

"Oh?" They pointed their finger at the bar.

Ben sat there. Well, his future self did. He had doubled in size, and his hair was white and wild, as was his beard. He was swaying in his seat as he slammed his hand down on the bar, calling over... was that Bobby? No. It couldn't be.

No, though, it was. He looked haggard.

"Are you sure, Ben?"

"More!" Ben yelled.

Sighing, Bobby poured another drink and handed it to Ben, who drank it messily, part ending in his beard, part spilling down his shirt.

"I can't do this anymore," Bobby said. "Look around you, Ben. It's time to give this up."

"It's fine. It will get busy. Just you wait."

"Ben! It's midnight on a Saturday. There's no one coming. They've all moved on."

"No! People love it here. People love the gay bar! Just you wait."

"Goddamit, Ben. That was years ago. No one gives a shit about a gay bar anymore. When was the last time you really paid attention to the world out there? Kids today don't even define themselves as gay. They just date whomever."

"Don't you goddammit me! We made this space great once, and we will make it great again."

"No. Not we, Ben. I can't. I'm done."

Bobby walked out from behind the bar. Ben got off his bar stool to stop him, but Bobby pushed by. Ben fell to the ground.

"Don't you leave me!"

"Everyone already left, Ben. Get out yourself. Close this place, and sober up, and for god's sake, change your shirt."

"Don't you leave me!"

But Bobby had already left.

Disgusted, Ben watched his future self cry and rage and tantrum on the floor.

"Please, Avenir. This can't be my future."

"This? This one is far likelier than the last, and yet still, it is unlikely. A time without a gay bar? Yes, it will come, but not in your lifetime," they said. "Hatred still simmers everywhere, some of it not even in secret. Leaders are elected with agendas to return us to the Straight White Way. The wrong that is the right still lives, and as long as it does, there will be a need for places that are safe and inclusive." They paused. "Even if sometimes, even those places themselves fall victim to the vile violence outside. One day though, someday, the gay bar will be gone."

As the fog rolled in, the rainbow flag above the bar fell to the ground. Future Ben's incoherent sobs followed them into the grey.

"I fear that," he said. "That the bar will become nothing, and I won't be able to leave it."

"Yes."

"And I've seen so many bar owners turn into drunks. I worry about that too."

"Yes, I know."

"I don't want that to happen."

"You have control."

"So, I should quit the bar? Close it down now?"

"That's certainly an option."

"Should I?"

"I can't tell you what you should do."

"But what if..."

"What if. Yes. I can certainly show you many a what if."

The fog rolled in again.

This Future Ben wasn't as out of shape, but he still looked rough. He wasn't at the bar though. This was Ben's apartment, the same apartment he had now, although it was cluttered. No, not cluttered. It was filthy.

Ben lay on the couch, a remote control in his hand. He stared blankly at the television in front of him, no expression on his wrinkled face. The coffee table in front of him was covered in bags and boxes of half-eaten snacks, dirty plates and glasses, and a pile of pizza boxes under it. The air in the apartment was stale, a dozen odors combining.

The phone rang. Ben didn't stir.

"Do you want to hear the message?"

Ben turned to Avenir. "Do I?"

Avenir shrugged, but sure enough, Ben could suddenly hear his own voice, as if he had a phone to his ear.

"This is Ben. Don't leave a message. I won't call back."

"Ben! It's Bobby and Tina. Call us. We are worried sick. It's been three weeks."

"Three weeks," Future Ben thought aloud. "How can it already be three weeks? Still, they're fine. Everyone's fine. No one needs me. They worry. It's cute that they worry. But I'm fine too. This is all I need. Just me. I can only rely on me. All I need is me. I'm fine. Not lonely at all. Not. At. All."

Future Ben closed his eyes, and a fat tear rolled down his pale cheek.

Ben turned to Avenir. "Please. Are there no possible futures that are happy?"

That's what he suspected of course. That in the end, everyone died broken and alone. That everything else was just delay of the inevitable. That pride, and all that went with it, was a glittery gay distraction before death.

"Is that why you don't celebrate?" Avenir asked. "Because it's pointless?"

Is that why, Ben thought, as the fog swirled away with them in it again. It wasn't that it was too corporate, or too mainstream, or too busy. Those were just excuses, he knew that. And it wasn't Jake. That was just an excuse too, one he knew he could get away with.

Really, was it getting anywhere? All the years, all the parades, all the bars, all the protests and marches and campaigns, was any of it actually making a difference in the world?

"That's the question, isn't it?" Avenir said, and the fog rolled away once more.

It was Good Judy's, and by the look of Bobby behind the bar, it was a not so distant future. A man came in, in his thirties perhaps. He looked nervous. He wasn't particularly handsome. He was just a man. Bobby smiled at him, as Bobby did. The man smiled back and approached the bar.

"Can I get you a drink?" Bobby said.

"Please," the man said. "A beer. Doesn't matter what."

Bobby slid a bottle across the bar top. "New here?"

"New to all of this," the man said. "This is my first time in a..."

"Gay bar?"

The man chuckled. "You say it so easily. I'm not... I'm not out."

"Well, have a seat at the bar," Bobby said. "While you're getting comfortable, you can keep my company."

Bobby was amazing like that, making people feel at home. That's what Good Judy's was. That's what any good gay bar should be: a home to anyone, regardless of gender or age or orientation or appearance, regardless of whether they were out or in, or somewhere in between.

Ben watched Bobby chat with the new man, who introduced himself as Andy. Ben smiled. He liked seeing things like this. Yes, it was Bobby doing it, but Ben was providing the...

He caught his breath and his thoughts stopped. Into the bar walked Kevin, hand in hand with someone else. Someone more his age. Yes. A much better match.

"You don't need to convince me," Avenir said. "But you sound like you're convincing yourself."

"Too young," Marc said, suddenly appearing next to Avenir.

"And too handsome," said the other Marsha.

"All three? Ganging up now, are we?"

"No one waits for anyone, Ben," Avenir said. "Not forever."

"I never asked him to wait. I never asked for anything."

Hadn't he though? Hadn't he wanted Kevin to wait? Wasn't it nice to have someone pining away for him, even if he was never going to act on it?

"You tell us," Marc said.

"I..."

Fog rolled in and Good Judy's was gone, and then it was just Ben and Avenir, and the sun was beating down on another parade. They were standing in the crowd, and people were laughing and smiling and shouting to friends.

"What is this now?" Ben asked.

There was Kevin, still hand in hand with the same man, but they were older now, and there were rings on their fingers.

There was Bobby, and he was kissing Andy, and Andy was kissing him back, even in this public gay throng.

Floats passed back, sports teams and church groups and bars and diners, and giant corporations proclaiming their rainbow capitalism and their affirmation of all things LGBTQ* (or whatever the acronym had evolved into in this timeline. Maybe one day, there was will be a word that encompasses all genders and orientations. Maybe there already is. We like the sound of 'people').

"Just a parade," Ben said. "Yes, they're getting their happy endings. I see that." He looked around. "Where am I though?" he asked. "Isn't this my vision quest or whatever it is." Music filled the air, pride anthems old and new, mingling together.

"Look," Avenir said.

Behind them, behind the crowd, a boy walked, holding a girl's hand. The girl snickered and pointed at someone in the crowd, and the boy's face flushed. She pointed at something else, and laughed a bit louder, and the louder she laughed, the deeper was the flush in his cheeks. He pulled his hand from hers.

"What's wrong, Micah?" she asked.

"I just don't think you should point and laugh."

"Why not? They're all so weird."

"What if... what if someone you knew was out there though? What if your brother was? What if I was?"

"Don't be silly, Micah. We've been dating for two years. I know you're not like them." She waved dismissively at the crowds.

"Yes, I am!" Micah cried out. "I'm gay, Cathy. I've always been gay!"

The fog rolled in, covering the shocked expression on her face, and the tears racing down his.

"This parade," Avenir said, "it gave him the courage to come out. How many others does it help, seeing that they are not alone? Seeing love celebrated not shunned?"

Ben couldn't speak. He remembered being in the closet, as long ago as it was. He remembered the freedom he felt the first time in a gay space, the magnificence of that first parade, the magic of that first gay dance floor.

The fog rolled in.

"I..."

"Don't say anything," Avenir said. "One more stop."

The fog was replaced by a house. It was just an average little house. On the couch sat a man, in a white shirt stained with grease and sweat. He was watching sports and had a beer in hand. On the wall hung a crucifix.

"Max?" a woman entered the room, and the man grunted. "Max, can you mute the TV? Micah wants to talk to us."

In came the boy from the street. Oh no, Ben thought. He had seen this too many times. Everything about the scene screamed at him. This man on the couch, this Max with his football and his Jesus, he wouldn't understand. Ben's heart ached for what Micah was about to experience.

"Mom, Dad," the boy said, staring down at his feet. "I have something I wanted to tell you guys."

"Spit it out, boy, the game is on."

Don't do it, Micah, Ben thought. Wait. Wait until you're older.

He couldn't be more than fourteen really. Old enough to know who he was, certainly, but not necessarily old enough to know what it meant, especially to people like his father.

"I think I'm gay," he said, and Ben caught his breath in his throat, wanting to step from the vision into the house and stop what he was sure was about to happen.

Max looked at his son. “So? You like boys. That's fine.”

Micah looked up, and there was such light behind his teary eyes.

“You don't hate me?”

“Micah, you are everything your mother and I could have wanted -” the mother was standing behind her husband, hands on his shoulder, and she was smiling and nodding along – “all we care about is you being happy and safe. And being quiet during the game!” Max laughed, and Micah joined in with him, as the fog rolled over.

They were in Ben's office. “More and more often,” Avenir said, “that is what will happen. And one day, Micah will grow up, and he will meet a man he loves, and he will tell their children about a time when people cared about other people's sexual orientation, and the children will laugh about the strange olden days.”

Ben turned to Avenir, and he too had tears in his eyes. “That's a future I want to see,” he said.

Avenir smiled, a smile that flickered from face to face. They were right though, Ben had gotten used to it.

Ben had gotten used to a lot, he guessed. Including being alone.

“Just because you're used to something,” they said, “doesn't mean it's good for you.” Avenir stepped into the fog, as it thickened, thickened, thickened.

Ben opened his eyes. The clock read nine. He ran out of the office, checking his phone as he did. It was

Saturday morning still. The parade would just be lining up now. If he ran, he could probably catch it.

But, Ben was also gay and wasn't about to set foot in his first parade in years in the clothes he had slept in all night. Not to mention, his hair and his breath were both atrocious, no doubt. No, first, he would stop by his apartment and shower and change, and then he would just have to run a bit faster.

The Good Judy's float that year was just pulling out of the loading area when he arrived, out of breath but definitely freshened up. He hopped onto the float, to the surprised cheers of the staff and customers gathered on it. Tiny threw her arms around him and he hugged her back. He wouldn't cry though.

He looked at Bobby, and Bobby was smiling.

“Good,” Bobby mouthed at him.

Ben smiled, and the music suddenly came on. He knew this song. It was a song they always played on their float, a song everyone in the thousands of people watching the parade would know. It was an anthem of freedom and celebration and strength, and it was sung by a fierce diva that had all the gays swaying along.

Ben closed his eyes and lost himself in the anthem. When he opened his eyes, he saw, in the crowd, Jake's ghost, and the ghost was smiling. Now, tears came to Ben's eyes, happy tears that he blinked away. When they were gone, so was Jake, and Ben knew he wouldn't see him again.

More, he knew he wouldn't need to.

But wait, there, where the ghost had stood, stood Kevin, and Ben leapt off the float.

"Boss!" Tiny called.

"Where are you going?" Bobby yelled.

Ben crossed the street to where Kevin was waving at him, a broad smile on his face. "I thought you didn't do Pride," Kevin said, as Ben approached him.

"I thought I didn't either," Ben said. "Do you want to be on a float with me?" He held out his hand, and smiled proudly as Kevin took it.

As they ran back to the float, Ben shouted to the crowd, "happy pride!"

Pride Anthems

(in no particular order)

A pride anthem is a song that celebrates the struggles and triumphs of the LGBT* community. Many of the list below are sung by divas whose vocals will fill the dance floors at your local bar. Some are slower, emphasizing perhaps the other side of the community, a side that has survived loss and grief and rejection. The perseverance that those songs showcase contributes to the unity, affirmation, and celebration essential for a great anthem.

There's certainly other songs, and I'd love to hear what your favorite anthems are. Get in touch on social media and let's talk Pride!

1. We R Who We R – Ke$ha: Released in 2010, this song was written in response to an epidemic of bullying that led to the suicides of many LGBT youth.
2. It's Raining Men – The Weather Girls: Released originally in 1982, this camp classic is a must-play for any pride celebration. The 90s remake features RuPaul.
3. Same Love – Macklemore & Ryan Lewis feat. Mary Lambert: Hip hop culture may be stereotypically homophobic, but this song started to change that, being adopted as an anthem for the same-sex marriage campaign in Washington State in 2012.

4. Dancing Queen – ABBA: There's an euphoria that comes from this beloved disco hit. From 1976 to now, it's guaranteed to make queens dance.
5. People Like Us – Kelly Clarkson: This 2013 release from the first American Idol is another celebration of hope. We may all be misfits, but we're together.
6. Firework – Katy Perry: Released in 2010, this song's message of empowerment comes across so beautifully in the music video.
7. Express Yourself – Madonna: Every list of pride anthems has to include this 1989 track. Madonna's support of the LGBT community has run throughout her career and this song, with its message of speaking out for what you want and who you are, is a classic example of that support translating into music.
8. Born This Way – Lady Gaga: Many people have drawn connections between this song and Express Yourself, but this 2011 release from Mother Monster is even clearer in its support of minorities standing up and being affirmed.
9. I Want To Break Free – Queen: A cross-dressing video accompanying this song's 1984 release was a slap in the face to the patriarchy. Lead singer Freddy Mercury's flamboyance cements this song as a challenge to oppression.
10. Finally – CeCe Peniston: Arguably one of the biggest dance classics of all time, this 1991 song captures the feeling of freedom that happens after coming out.
11. We Are Family – Sister Sledge: Often rejected by their own families, many LGBT people recognize the importance of "chosen" family. This 1979 disco hit sums up perfectly the support and celebration that that chosen family can provide.

12. Be As – Prozzak: This 2000 release from a Canadian duo celebrates individuality, self-expression, and freedom.
13. Raise You Up / Just Be– Kinky Boots: Cyndi Lauper and Harvey Fierstein collaborated on this 2012 musical, which teaches the lesson that only by exposing our differences can we find our similarities.
14. Smalltown Boy – Bronski Beat: This 1984 song and video tell the story of a gay boy, bullied and rejected by his family and society.
15. A Little Respect – Erasure: Out songwriter Andy Bell wrote this 1988 release, which asks for respect not only from a lover, but from the greater world.
16. Freedom! 90 – George Michael: Although this song may have been more about its singer's new-found freedom from Wham, it can easily be heard as a coming out song too. Michael came out officially in 1998, and was an advocate for LGBT rights until his 2016 death.
17. YMCA – Village People: Campy and colorful, this disco hit showcases gay uniform fantasies of the '70s, and references how gay men would often cruise YMCA, among other gyms (and bars, and bathhouses, and parks, and churches, and anywhere really!)
18. Raise Your Glass – P!nk: In 2010, Pink released this track, a tribute to everyone who is "wrong in all the right ways." It became an immediate anthem for dirty little freaks everywhere.
19. Sissy That Walk – RuPaul: Drag Race has taken the artform of drag and mainstreamed it. RuPaul, inarguably the most successful drag queen of all time, released this fierce track in 2014.

20. Closer to Fine – Indigo Girls: No list of pride anthems would be complete without this lesbian duo and their 1989 single about the journey to self-acceptance.
21. Don't Leave Me This Way – Thelma Houston: This massive 1976 disco hit was re-released in the mid 90s, and was not only a great club track but also one heavy with significance for gay men bearing the daily grief that was the height of the AIDS epidemic.
22. Beautiful – Christina Aguilera: This 2002 single quickly resonated with the LGBT community for its themes of self-empowerment and inner beauty.
23. True Colors – Cyndi Lauper: Although not written by Lauper, this 1986 single became a gay standard. The True Colors Fund, co-founded by Lauper in 2008, focuses on educating people on LGBT issues and ending LGBT youth homelessness.
24. I Will Survive – Gloria Gaynor: One of the best-known disco songs, this song symbolizes the resilience of both individuals and the greater community.
25. I'm Coming Out – Diana Ross: Although the coming out in this 1980 song refers more to the debutante process, it certainly can also represent the celebration and freedom of telling the world who you are.
26. Free – Ultra Nate: Its theme of freedom made this 1997 dance track an immediate hit with the LGBT community.
27. Go West – Pet Shop Boys: This 1992 cover of a Village People song was first performed at an AIDS charity event. Lyrically, it seems pretty obvious: leave the square states where you're hated and come to the coast (San Francisco) where you can be free.

28. All The Lovers – Kylie Minogue: This 2010 hit for the Australian pop diva had a video celebrating sexuality, including same-sex couples. It also recognizes the role past relationships have in making us who we are.
29. Last Dance – Donna Summer: Although Summer's relationship with the gay community has been rocky at times, this 1978 disco anthem has resonated with gay men for its catchy rhythm and its message of continuing to celebrate in the face of adversity.
30. Last Party – MIKA: The self-identified bisexual artist captures the nearly mythic story of Freddy Mercury's last party in this 2015 track. We're left with a haunting and beautiful musical memory.
31. Come To My Window – Melissa Etheridge: The first track to be released after her coming out, this 1993 song tells a story of secret loves finally ready to break free.
32. Closer – Tegan and Sara: Openly lesbian sisters, Tegan and Sara deliver an ode to the excitement and heat of adolescent attraction with this 2012 single.
33. Constant Craving – kd lang: The ache of the closet runs through every note of this 1992 single from the out Canadian singer.
34. Make Your Own Kind of Music – Mama Cass: This 1969 hit from Mama and Papas singer perhaps gains its spot on this list from the soundtrack to 1996's Beautiful Thing. Still, lyrically it speaks to being true to yourself.
35. Proud – Heather Small: The artists's first single was released in 2000, as gay people were finding their way into everyone's homes via Showtime's Queer As Folk.
36. Relax – Frankie Goes To Hollywood: Sexual innuendo in the lyrics and promotional material helped make this 1983 release extremely popular in gay clubs.

37. You Make Me Feel – Sylvester: A combination of a falsetto singing voice and a certain flamboyant androgyny, this out singer scored a huge hit with this 1978 release.
38. She Keeps Me Warm – Mary Lambert: Openly lesbian artist Mary Lambert collaborated with Macklemore on Same Love (above) and went on to release this 2013 celebration of sexuality.
39. Girls and Boys – Blur: This 1994 British rock track bent gender and sexuality and became a bi/pan-sexual rallying cry.
40. Wild – Troye Sivan: This 2015 release from South-African born Sivan shows that even though the world may have changed so much for kids coming out today (Sivan came out at 15), one thing remains consistent with out singers from years before: love makes us all wild.

A tale of sex, drugs, kidnapping, and brunch.

Go down the rabbit hole with Alex in this story of suspense and sexcapades. Alex's boyfriend has gone missing, and Alex and friends don't know where to start. Is it the Caterpillar, whose drugs get them high? Is it the Walrus, whose hate is loud and vocal? Or is there someone else, somewhere in the gayborhood, somewhere in the crowd of dancers the a club known as Wonderland?

Things get curiouser and curiouser for Alex when his past returns to haunt him.

In Wonderland, it is easy to drink me, eat, me, sniff me, do me, and Alex is going along with it, too lost in his own pain and regret. Maybe what Alex needs is a trip out of the gayborhood and back to his hometown, but when that trip is with his ex anything can happen.

Rob Browatzke is a teller of stories and thrower of parties. You can find him on all sorts of social media, and stalking him there is welcome!

www.browatzke.com

Made in the USA
Lexington, KY
16 May 2018